LIFE HACKS OF DELHI

ROHIT ROHILLA

BlueRose ONE.com
Stories Matter

First Published in March 2022

ISBN: 978-93-5611-113-4

BLUEROSE PUBLISHERS
www.BlueRoseONE.com
info@bluerosepublishers.com
+91 8882 898 898

Cover Design:
Akash Bartwal

Typographic Design:
Ilma

Distributed by: BlueRose, Amazon, Flipkart

Preface

I am exploring Delhi for quite some time now. It's loud but also silent, it's cruel but also kind. I have accepted it the way it is. But there's something about this city that makes me want to know more and more about it. I have always been fond of books. I never thought I would write one, but as soon as I decided to write one, I knew it had to be about Delhi. This city has some sort of magic in its air.

Delhi has always been a go-to place for tourists as well as Indians. For tourists, it's a great place in terms of monuments, food, and culture, but for Indians, it's great in terms of getting a job, for competitive exam practices, and earning money.

I have been noticing this city for quite some time now; the places, the habits, the people, everything. This book is like a friend you didn't know you needed. It has everything for you assembled in a few pages. Having it in your hand wouldn't make you feel, even for the slightest second, that you don't know this city. It has a couple of chapters, and each one of them imparts some knowledge. This book will always be special to me; it's a part of me. It's all those things I wish someone had told me. Writing this book hasn't been less of a roller coaster. Bringing everything that I have known until now and assembling them in a few pages so that the readers out there can be helped in some way wasn't easy, but for sure it was worth it.

I hope reading the book is worth your time. In case you have any comments or suggestions on the book, please feel free to email me at rohitrohilla132@gmail.com. I would love to hear from you.

Acknowledgement

My greatest appreciation is for my parents, who supported me throughout the whole journey and helped in bringing this book to life. I wouldn't have been able to write this book without my parent's endless support. They played a leading role and inspired me to write a book. I never thought I would be writing the acknowledgment for my book someday, but here I am. I guess good things take time.

I would like to thank my friends. There were a lot of challenges that I had to face while writing this book, but none of them felt too big because my friends were there for me at every stage, helping and guiding me with their knowledge.

My greatest heartfelt thanks will always be to Delhi, the city that taught me a lot of things, the city that saw me failing, succeeding, laughing, and overall growing day by day. You made me the person that I am today. Delhi, this book wouldn't have been possible without you. Thank you for giving me memories that I will cherish forever.

I am thankful to my editor, who read the manuscript a couple of times and gave me valuable suggestions throughout the journey of writing this book.

This acknowledgment can't be completed without expressing my gratitude towards my readers who hold this book. Thank you for choosing this book and allowing me to do what I love! I hope this book helps you in some way or another.

Author's Page

The author has always been a bibliophile and loved his books a bit too much. He is currently majoring in Philosophy and Political Science from Delhi university and has an interest in studying law in the future. This book is a dream come true for the author, as he never thought that one fine day he would be writing his own book and sharing his perspective with the world.

For the author, books, words, and expressions matter a lot. Life Hacks of Delhi is his first book. And with this book as a debut, the author is ready to start off his journey.

Cotents

Accommodation

1. If you are looking for some rented accommodation (Flat, PG or Room), take it close to a Metro station. It will help you plan your travel better.

2. While taking a rented accommodation, usually the property dealer will ask for 1 month of rent as his commission. Please use your negotiation skills here. If lucky, you can save some money here.

3. Food in PG & Tiffin is usually neither good nor hygienic & you pay a lot for this food. If you are living alone, learn the art of cooking, you can have the food of your choice which is healthy & good. If you are living in PG or with friends, hire a maid to cook, at least you will have better food to eat.

4. A family of 4 people (Husband, Wife, 2 School-going Kids) may find it easy to live in Delhi with a monthly expense of 30–40K, if you have simple lifestyle and preferences.

These are the most posh areas of the city that is meant only for super rich and then goes down.

1. NDMC Area: Truly, this is the place offering the best quality of life in India. The entire municipality is composed of only and only super posh areas. Some of these areas are India Gate bungalows, housing politicians and Chanakyapuri, Jor Bagh, Golf links, Lodi Road and a lot more. The roads are green and clean, all metro lines are underground, and no encroachments are there on roads. Also, lots of parks, huge bungalows, luxury hotels and clubs

are there in close vicinity. There is a huge golf course, most stadiums of the city, and the two markets: Connaught Place and Khan Market are only meant for shopping of elites.

You need to be a billionaire to live here.

2. South Delhi: Just a bit south are more posh areas. Though this area is not well planned, but far more lively compared to peaceful Centre. Some of the posh areas here are RK Puram, Vasant Vihar, Greater Kailash, Hauz Khas, New Friends Colony and Defense ColonLike central Delhi, these localities also enjoy a lot of similar amenities. This area has most of the malls and markets of the city, so plenty of shopping options. Pollution is a problem here unlike central Delhi, as main roads get choked in peak hours.

Now the places for middle class:

Dwarka sub city: Very liveable place in West Delhi with low floor apartments, parks and fresh air compared to interior of the city. Shopping areas are in vicinity and it is now connected well to the city by metro.

West Delhi: Other areas good to live in west Delhi are Janakpuri, Rajouri Garden, Paschim Vihar, Peeragadhi and Punjabi Bagh. These all are planned colonies with good amenities for middle class people.

Rohini and adjoining areas: Another sub city like Dwarka in northern part of city, just same as Dwarka. The nearby areas of Pitampura, Model Town and Shalimar Bagh are also good to live.

Parts of East Delhi: East Delhi is mostly polluted and crowded, but there are some good areas here. Mayur

Vihar, Preet Vihar, Nirman Vihar and Yamuna Vihar are among quite a few good planned livable areas in trans Yamuna area.

In NCR region, Only Noida and Greater Noida are the places that can be considered good which provide a high standard of living for middle class. Some sectors equivalent to posh areas in Delhi located in Noida are 14, 14A, 15, 15A, 17, 21, 23, 24, 25, 26, 27, 30, 31, 33, 34, 35, 36, 37, 39, 40, 41, 44, 50, 51, 52, 53, 55 and 56.

Note:- But the area I described makes up hardly 25% of Delhi Urban area. I will suggest that one from a high or middle class income shall stay within limits of these areas only, otherwise you will live among poor with pollution problems, no parks and poor sanitation.

Transportation

If you want to use public transportation, go for Ola or Uber. Since you are a non Delhite, the auto wala will get that by your accent and will overcharge for sure.

The best one is to get a metro card and prefer metro over any other modes of transport because it is cheap, convenient and keeps you safe from Delhi's pollution.

Delhi Metro connects the entirety of Delhi and parts of NCR (Gurgaon, Noida, Faridabad, Ghaziabad) with 296 km of track length and 214 stations.

You can also use E-rickshaw and DTC buses because it is CHEAPER than metro. (A woman can travel free in DTC buses, she can buy a ticket if she can afford.

Delhi Metro hacks:

Lifts: There are special lifts for physically challenged people at every metro station. Everyone can use them to avoid the rush at stairs or escalator. The best part is they are located at the nearest place of security checkpoints. I used this trick to avoid climbing 3 storeys at Anand Vihar Station.

Hidden Charging Points: Try to find wall fans at metro station. They are located at each station. Most of them are not working but the socket in which they are plugged in always works. You can use them as charging points. I have seen people doing it and i have also tried it myself. (Don't forget to put back the fan plug in socket).

Empty coaches: 8 th coach of every train is generally empty because it too far and most of the crowd stops at the distance of 6 th coach. (Last coaches are generally empty).

2nd coach of most of the train is also empty as men avoid going into that coach because it is next to women coach. They move towards other coaches with their friends or colleagues.

Use the Wall: If you are boarding from Rajiv chowk or Kashmiri gate. Board from the centre of platform as there is a wall on the side of the platform and because of that wall most crowd gets separated on both the sides of wall. Thus the coach you will board it will be less crowded than other coaches.

Even in this picture you can see there is less crowds on wall side as compared to open side.

Best standing places: The centre of the coach is generally empty because people always stick near to the gate. It's better to stand in the centre as there are rods and you can use them as back support. One of the most loved places by young people is next to door and getting the back support from the glass. No one gets disturbed and most importantly no one disturbs you.

(Just like the girl standing in black jeans and white t-shirt)

Free Space: I call it Free Space of metro train because it is one of the best places inside Delhi metro coaches if you are travelling for long distance and don't have a seat.

In between the coaches there is place to sit, stand and do whatever you want to do. You can read a book peacefully, listen to music, and watch a movie without even getting annoyed or annoying people.

It is also the best place for couples as there is enough space. Most of the people are focusing on outside world and listening to the name of stations. Both of them can stand there easily. They can talk and do stuff easily.

Helpful tips:-

1. Blue Line: If you are travelling from Dwarka-21 to New Delhi or any other railway station which comes after Rajeev Chowk and you want to save time, then rather than travelling in a normal metro which has 30 station, you can travel through AIRPORT EXPRESS LINE which has only 5 stations but the cost is 54 INR till New Delhi and it will take hardly 30 mins whereas, through normal metro it will take about 80 mins.

2. Never wait for trains near stairs of station. Most of the people wait there. Go to the end near girls bogie. Crowd is lesser and due to presence of girls, many behave nicely.

3. Always buy smart cards. Even if you are not frequent traveller. It saves from boredom of standing in queue.

4. If you are one station near to the terminal stations, start the journey from terminal station. Benefit - you will get a seat to sit for your entire journey.

5. Take stairs when lot of people take escalators. You will be probably first ones to exit without wasting time in queue for exit.

6. Dont leave your earphones connected to your mobile phones when not in use. The wire of earphones are used to pull the phones out of pocket in (extreme)rush hours. Result: You are only left with earphones.

In the end, I would like to say that Delhi Metro is the lifeline of over 2 million people. It is air-conditioned, cost-efficient, accessible and extremely clean, please do not try to damage/litter it. It is one of the best things to have happened to Delhi and it is only with the cooperation of travelers will it continue to be a world-renowned transport system. Having spent 2 hours in the metro everyday in the last few years and having countless experiences and a sense of attachment to the metro, this is my request to all those who use it.

To make the journey more convenient you may download this app - Delhi Bus & Delhi Metro Route.

It's a best app for DTC Busses and Delhi Metro. This app can guide you through the routes and lines of the metro. All you have to do is put in your start and end station, and the app tells you everything from the route, the amount of time it takes, and even alternative routes, if you might need them.

Tip:- If you find one light green, chances are that there you will find almost all of it green and if you find one light red, chances are that there you will find almost all the lights red.

Note:- Drive here with common sense. It will sound unbelievable, but try to be patient on Delhi road and follow lane driving.

Safety

- Avoid any possible brawl on roads and in pubs. Guns are very common here and you never know who has it under his belt. Just ignore if possible. If you get into serious trouble, just Call 100, Delhi Police is quite responsive and will be helpful.
- If you see a car with, Vidhayak, Police written on it try and maintain a distance. The driver is most likely to be looking for someone with whom he can share the question " janta hai mera bap kaun hai " so it will eat around 20 minutes of your time.
- Phone snatching here is very common try to keep your phone in the opposite side of the ongoing traffic, if you're walking. This means that if you're walking on a footpath and traffic is on your right, then keep your phone on the left side, while on a call
- Whenever you have to leave your belongings in car such as Laptop, iPad etc. always keep them in car trunk, they should not be visible from windows, otherwise within a minute the glass will be broken and you will find it missing.
- Check your purse and phone at constant intervals(sounds nerdy, right!) and avoid crowded areas. Keep your precious belongings (like extra jewellery or bling) at home or in bank lockers (safer than your house).

- Never trust strangers because you never know who's going to pick pocket or steal your stuff and when he/she's going to do it.
- Don't entertain strangers for too long if they seem suspicious (like if they keep glancing at uryour watch, purse or other expensive items).
- Don't go along showing off because that makes you a potential target in the thief's eyes.
- In the worst case scenario, if you are confronted and forced to fight, look tough and fight like you are fighting for your precious life.

For Girls

- Always carry a pepper spray in your bag at all times it gives you a sense of safety.
- Try avoiding walking on lonely streets alone, especially at nights. It's definitely not fair, and I hate to write this, but in the unfortunate state our city is in at the moment, you have to take such precautions.
- Avoid meeting in person, your online friends whom you don't know beyond the web world.
- Avoid wearing expensive jewelry accessories that might trigger such criminal acts.

Tip: Learning self defence gives you an edge over those.

Note:- Road rages are very common here, so try not to be part of it

Relationship and dating

How to make friends if you are totally new !

• To make friends one needs to have a starting conversation with people. If you're a reading enthusiast then a library is a place where you can get this easily because people are eager to talk to somebody when they're taking a break after long hours of studying.

You can start a conversation just with, "what's this book you're reading ?

There are many libraries in Delhi, one of which is British Council library, CP. Here books are mainly from British authors as one of the purposes of the foreign councils is to promote the culture of their country. Most of the visitors are those preparing for various exams like UPSC or CA.

- Join a meditation course or yoga classes. There is Isha Yoga Foundation's Inner Engineering course in Sarojni Nagar. See if it interests you. There are some fun courses by Art of Living too.
- Join an NGO with a cause which is closer to your heart. CRY, Prayas, HelpAge India, World Vision, UNICEF to name a few. You will feel way better about yourself and the world, in the process meeting some fantastic selfless individuals.

- Find your passion, interests and search for same groups on [Find your people - Meetup]. In this app you can go to conferences, meetings, parties, bars, pubs or even can organize one event.
- Join a good gym and do treadmill with a girl next to you on the next machine. Run like a horse may be at 15 speed, If u run like that she will notice you workout really hard. Then Say hi to girls who are next to you on treadmill try to start conversation that you are kinda new in the gym.

Miscellaneous Tips

- If you are coming for a new job which has modest salary, then avoid making girlfriend for at least 1 year.
- For boys, Avoid trusting girls very easily. They can be very sweet and courteous for their agenda and boys often misunderstand this.
- For girls, be very cautious while choosing friends. Never fall for sweetness, courtesy, chivalry etc. People out here are very good in using these skills, but in reality they are something else.
- Some girls are only inspired by fake feminism. So maybe, she can put false allegations on you of harassing. (Do not panic and immediately tell your family members)
- Some boys only travel to touch you and to follow you. Don't ignore them and file a complaint to the metro official.

- Never argue with the girl of Hauz Khas. Some of them are truly inspired by Neha Dhupia.

Best dating locations !

After a couple of dates in the movies, been to India Gate and Old Fort, it seems like one has exhausted the possibilities of fresh venues for a date in Delhi. Does it? There is so much more that two people could do while out on a date in Delhi.

There are hundreds of dating locations in Delhi therefore I choose some of the best where you can spend quality time with your partner:

1. Fio and Magique, Garden of Five 5 Senses

If a walk on the paths meandering through the garden is not a stimulus for your budding romance, what is? Not just the abundant natural beauty, but the food on offer at the restaurants is also an absolute treat!

Fio has a date-perfect ambiance.

2. Parthsarathy Rocks, JNU

If you are lovers by nature and lovers of nature, this is the spot for you. It is Surrounded by green landscapes, you can enjoy a sunset sitting atop your majestic throne together.

3. Rose Cafe, Saket

Tucked away in the boring and dreary Said-ul-Ajab locality in Saket, this cheerful little cafe with lovely pastel Victorian interiors is just the place for a quiet romance.

4. The Garden Restaurant, Lodhi Garden

The Garden Restaurant offers beautiful seating amid the green canopy to converse with your date. It is touted as Delhi's best alfresco restaurant.

5. SKY Lounge, Connaught Place

A one of its kind lounge set with LED-lit furniture, this is the place for you if you like swanky places. And of course if you enjoy heights.

6. Delhi Haat, INA

It is all things Delhi and all things Indian. A stroll through Delhi haat can be quite refreshing for a date. Needless to say, the food stalls shall definitely be a stop.

7. Ridge Road, North Campus

A walk or drive on this deserted road is definitely romantic. Where else can one find such a quiet spot in Delhi? This area also has several monuments like the Mutiny Memorial and the Baoli near Pir Ghaib, which can be explored.

8. Summer House Cafe, Aurobindo Place

The Aurobindo complex is brimming with places you can meet your date at. Summer House is one such place. It is not just beautiful but also happening with a line up of live music and performances.

9. Cafe Lota, Pragati Maidan

After exploring Pragati Maidan, Crafts Museum and Old fort, you and your date should land up at this absolute delightful cafe. The food will accompany your conversations gracefully.

10. Blue Frog, Mehrauli

If you want music to be a feature of your date, this is the place for you! The decor is urban and colorful, which will add to the glam-quotient of your date.

My Personal favourite

Champa Gali - It's a couple of hundred square yards of area, marked by a boundary wall that now houses multiple cafes/ restaurants and coffee shops.

This is how it looks like in the night:-

If you are a coffee person like me, you HAVE to visit Blue Tokai in the area. It is one of the best and the most authentic coffee experience. They serve excellent coffee and also host coffee making workshops.

This is how their outdoor area looks like –

It is located Some 300–400 meters behind the Saket Metro Station. If you are in the area, it is a must visit. The place also house Pho King which is a very good restaurant for a dinner/ lunch date.

Drinks and food

I have travelled around Delhi a fair bit, in quest of good food. In time, I began compiling a list of cheap and unique places which defined the character of the city on the gastronomical plane, according to me. In my selection, there are no well-known five star restaurants. I feel if you are in the city, you must cover what is peculiar to it, and found nowhere else.

1. Paranthe Wali Gali

The most well known parantha place in Delhi is this! It is at one of the off roads to Chandni Chowk. Not too expensive, but completely worth the price, the paranthas are fried and not to mention, leaving you wanting for more.

And this street vendor at Chandni Chowk is most famous for selling the yummiest sandwiches and besan ka cheela! Its a must visit when you're at Chandni Chowk!

2. Khan Omelette Corner

This 50 year old gem at Chawri Bazaar has managed to create a frenzy with its mouth watering variants of fried and boiled eggs. It can be a perfect snack for those of who're doing some serious shopping at Delhi. He opens only at 5 pm and it gets very crowded very soon.

3. Arjun Bombay Pav Bhaji

This place is know for serving the yummiest Pav Bhaji located in Model town, (try the Double Fried Pav Bhaji). You can also try their Vada Pavo. Arjun Pav Bhaji attracts 1000's of dedicated visitors in Delhi, making it a crowd favourite.

4. Hunger Strike

If Delhi is known for anything, it would be for the mouth watering momos! Hunger Strike in Lajpat Nagar is the go to place for just that. Their Tandoori Momos are a crowd favorite and honestly, they are to die for, all for just ₹ 90.

5. Chache Di Hatti

Just for ₹50 per plate, you get to enjoy some lip smacking, mouth watering and even mouth burning Chole Bhature, located in Kamla Nagar. This place gets sold out by 1pm, so if you want to eat some, go by 9:30!

6. Roshan Di Kulfi

Roshan Di Kulfi has been around for 50 years and still serves the best Kulfi Falooda located in Karol Bagh. They have 3 amazing flavours: Kesar Badam Pista, Mango and paan all for ₹115! You also get sugar-free versions for all those who are conscious!

7. Bitto Tikki Wala

What once started as a cart, with Tikkis so yummy, they became a franchise across the town. This is the best way to beat the winter! The tikkis are so yummy that you just can't stop with one plate.

8. North Campus

MOMOTARIAN. When you visit DU, this is the place to try out. Their yummy momos with butter chicken gravy is the crowd favourite.

9. Big Yellow Door

In the pic:- Baked Cheese Nachos. Their famous BYD Cheese Bomb burger and bat cheese nachos are a must try. And the best part is, being a restaurant near DU, its very affordable.

10. Khan Chacha

The famous Khan Market has Khan Chacha selling the yummiest Chicken Tikka and Chicken Tikka rolls. It gets packed very fast, so if you want to taste some of the yummi-ness, head there by late evening.

11. Art Of Spices

Very close to the Karol Bagh metro station, this place sells the best Malai Chicken Tikka and egg rolls. Its very budget friendly (₹300 for two) but you have to wait almost an hour for a place.

12. Kulcha King

Situated in Sarojini Nagar, Kulcha King serves the best Amritsari Kulcha and Chole. The price ranges from ₹70 to ₹150.

With this my food journey has come to an end. I am sure there are many I have missed but I have hand picked my favourite out of all the cuisines.

Tip:- There is a new concept here called Barshala where drinks are on MRP, like really true MRP and you can sit in and drink. Around 9 Barshala are there in Delhi.

Note:- There are very strict police guidelines regarding drinking in Delhi. Never drink around a wine shop, either arrange a car to drink in or drink at home.

Weekend % Touris

You can get every flavour in Delhi. Below are the places as per you mood.

If you are interested in the culture and history of Delhi you can visit the following places:

1. Humayun Tomb

Humayun's Tomb is UNESCO word heritage site, there are currently 3 UNESCO heritage sites in delhi and other two are Qutub Minar and Red Fort.

Humayun's Tomb is beautiful and resembles Tajmahal is certain way.

2. Majnu Ka Tila

Also called 'The Little Tibet', this place has been the house to the refugees from Tibet who followed their spiritual leader the great Dalai Lama into an exile in the country.

This section of North Delhi provides quite a vivid display of the Tibetan culture in the form of the temples, cafes, restaurants, bookshops and the guest houses that the place has.

3. Satputla Bridge

One of the most commendable hidden places in Delhi, the Satpula Bridge has held quite a significance in our history. This bridge which derives its name due to a collection of seven bridges was used for water harvesting in old days.

To add to its charm this place also acted as the wall for defence during the reign of Sultan Mohammed Shah Tughlaq.

4. Mirza Ghalib ki Haveli

This haveli was established in the memory of the world renowned Urdu poet Mirza Asadullah Baig Khan popularly called Mirza Ghalib. This place was his home during one of the most challenging years of his life and holds some of his exquisite works even today. This place has an in house museum which is now maintained by the Indian government.

5. Bhardwaj Lake Asola

As astonishing as it may sound the hustle bustle of a city like Delhi also has a hidden gem of a lake towards its southern end. Glorious in ways more than one, this lake sits in the Asola Wildlife Sanctuary, an area that is reserved by the Delhi Wildlife Department. And quite a number of the birds and animals can be spotted here.

6. Jahaz Mahal

The palace that goes by the name Jahaz Mahal is also among one of the hidden places in Delhi to visit. This place derives its name from its reflection that looks like a floating ship in the nearby lake.

7. Sanjay Van and Taudevi Lal

A city like Delhi which contains such large demographic has managed to maintain a lush green forest at its heart. This forest that spreads over 780 acres of land goes by the name Sanjay Van and is among one of the best-hidden places in Delhi to visit. It is a rising hub for jogging and cycling.

If you are religious types:

1. Lotus Temple

Lotus temple in Delhi is one of the seven Bahai worship temples across the world. Others are at Wilmette, Panama city, Sydney, Apia, Frankfurt and Kampala. As it's a worship place for all religions, the temple does not have any statue or image of any God or Goddes

2. Iskon Temple

Flocked by the devotees of Lord Krishna, people visit the temple grounds in search of contentment and serenity. Surrounded by hymns, prayers, chanting of devotees and faint chattering of people, there's calmness in the hustling of people over here, as no one seems to be in any sort of hurry. If you're seeking a place where you can reflect on important life questions, then this is where you should definitely land up.

3. Sacred Heart Cathedral

Among the oldest buildings in Delhi and one with exceptional architecture and design is the Sacred Heart Cathedral Church, Delhi. Sacred Heart tops the list of the most famous and followed churches in Delhi with Roman Catholic affiliation.

4. Swaminarayan Akshardham Temple

Narayan Sarovar is the main attraction of the temple. There are 108 faces of cows/gomukh laced along the lake,. It is believed that these 108 cow faces represent 108 Hindu Gods. The temple has 10 gates. What is more interesting is that all gates face the 10 directions as per Vedic literature.

5. Ahinsa Sthal

Ahinsa Sthal is a Jain temple located in Mehrauli, Delhi. The main deity of the temple is Mahavira, the 24th and last Tirthankara.

If you are college going or young at heart and like only fun stuff,

1. Codebreak 60 - Kamla Nagar

A real-life room escaping challenge where you are the live-sized players. Real-Lifean experience of being stuck in a game? This is it! The grand live size moto of "1 Hour 1 Team 1 Goal - Escape" if You can run and chill through your body. The experience is crazy and wild and a must try once in your life.

2. Mystery Rooms, Rajouri Garden

It is a challenging race against the clock where the sole motive is to get yourself out of a theme based room before time kicks you out. This is one game that will challenge all your senses.

3. Barney's Den - Hauz Khas

They have great equipment which is comfortable for all age groups and offers games for beginners and pro-level laser tag players making it one of the best places to visit with your friends. With around 17 different game options that you can enjoy with your group of friends (minimum 3).

4. PaintBall

Are you waiting for a game to get a chance to just shoot somebody? (Not literally!) Then you already know that the colorful, cheerful and crazy game of paintball is the right thing for you. For a fresher or even a well-seasoned paintballer, Delhi has many arena options for paintball. Whichever's closest, pick the one.

5. Indian Mountaineering Foundation - South Campus

Food, Coffee, Video Games, Clubbing, Books - Every Delhiite's outdoor activities surprisingly. If you want to be adventurous for a day and not spend days, money and hours trekking or going to mountains for adventure sports then worry not, Delhi also has the facilities for you.

6. Delhi Eye - Kalindi Kunj

The wheel has 36 air-conditioned cabins, each able to carry six passengers, from which Akshardham Temple, Humayun›s Tomb, Lotus Temple, Qutb Minar and Red Fort are visible on a clear day. This is surely a true marvel in itself.

7. SMAAASH

For the ultimate gaming experience, the SMAAASH alley is up top. Not only gaming but for bowling, go-karting, cricket and other things too, SMAAASH is a futuristic indoor entertainment place that you'll definitely get hooked to and for sure wouldn't want to get out of. The place also has a food parlor inside to satisfy your food cravings.

Shopping

There are so many options when it comes to shopping. Delhi has a variety of markets starting from clothes that includes wedding outfits, college wear, winters and many more

1. Connaught Place

The busiest of all the shopping places of Delhi is Connaught Place. This shopping place looks great with its white appearance. You will find the outlets of all brands here at the same point within a distance of few steps. The well organized showrooms and stores of Connaught Place offers a range of classy fabric, jewelry, Indian books, handcraft items, electronic goods and more.

How to Reach: Metro (Rajiv Chowk Metro Station)

What to Buy: Clothes, jewelry, books, Indian handcraft items, electronic products and more

2. Palika Bazaar

This shopping plaza is situated at the center of Connaught Place and is fully air-conditioned. Delhiites and people visiting Delhi from other region of India purchase clothes, perfumes, accessories, footwear, electronic products, CDs and many other products from Palika Bazaar. One should have the ability to bargain to get the products at reasonable prices. This place is well connected through all modes of public transport such as buses, taxies, autos and metro.

How to Reach: Metro (Rajiv Chowk Metro Station)

What to Buy: Clothes, perfumes, accessories, footwear, electronic goods, CDs

3. Janpath

Janpath is a popular local market of Delhi that offers a lot of things. People of all ages and taste can pick something of their choice from Janpath Market. The shops of Janpath offer goods from Tibet and all over India. It is a good place to shop souvenirs and many other useful things. To get the products at decent price one requires bargaining skills. As the market always remains overcrowded, one has to be careful regarding their wallets, pockets and purses

How to Reach: Metro (Janpath Metro Station)

What to Buy: Traditional and western clothes, accessories, footwear, antiques, handicrafts, paintings, leather work, cheap jewelry, etc.

4. Sarojini Market

Sarojini Nagar offers range of fashionable clothes at cheap rates. From apparel to kitchenware, accessories to household items, you will get everything in this market. To get the trendiest of things you can opt for Sarojini Market. But you should have good capability of bargaining within you to get your product at decent price. Teenagers and people following trend love to shop from this market.

How to Reach: Metro (INA Metro Station)

What to Buy: Apparel, accessories, household items, kitchenware, electronic products.

5. Lajpat Nagar Market

Lajpat Nagar Market is popular for offering all types of formal and casual wear. It is popular for offering garments at reasonable prices especially traditional Indian dresses like saris and salwar kameezes. Besides, you can also pick good quality footwear, accessories and bags from Lajpat Nagar Market. Trendy boys and girls can pick their kind of goods from this shopping place. Not only this, you can also pick furnishing and decor products from the stores of Lajpat Market.

How to Reach: Metro (Lajpat Nagar Metro Station)

What to Buy: Garments, accessories, footwear, bags, home furnishing and d□or items

6. Karol Bagh Market

One of the oldest shopping areas is Karol Bagh. It is popularly known for offering an array of gorgeous bridal wears and traditional Indian garments. Besides, cosmetics, books, shoes, gadgets and electronic items are the things you can grab from the market places. There are some well known shopping places around Karol Bagh like Ajmal Khan Road (known for inexpensive readymade), Ghaffar (popular for imported good), Arya Samajh Road (visited for second hand books) and Bank Street (popular for gold jewelry).

How to Reach: Metro (Karol Bagh Metro Station)

What to Buy: Bridal wear, cosmetics, books, shoes, gadgets and electronic items

7. Khan Market

Khan market is regarded as one of the posh shopping places in Delhi. This specially designed U-shaped market has well organized book shops, showrooms of branded clothes, boutiques and stores offering classy lifestyle items.

How to Reach: Metro (Khan Market Metro Station)

What to Buy: Garments, books, lifestyle items, food items

8. Dilli Haat

Dilli Haat is a colorful shopping place that offers traditional handicrafts and handlooms from the villages of India. Therefore, it is named as Dilli Haat because it is set up in a manner Indian village markets are set up. You will get the ultimate feel of Indian villages as the shops resembles like thatched roof cottages. Besides purchasing pottery, jewelry, saris and paintingS.

How to Reach: Metro (INA Metro Station)

What to Buy: Jewelry, paintings, fabrics, saris, pottery, furniture and many more.

9. Chandni Chowk

Chandni Chowk is one of the most popular shopping places in Delhi. Tough the winding lanes of this area are untidy and congested, yet people visit this place for purchasing inexpensive things like wedding lehengas, embroidered bags, semi-precious jewelry, silk and cotton clothes. One can also buy books and electronic products from Chandni Chowk. Do satisfy your taste buds by tasting the traditional food from the stalls of culinary lanes.

How to Reach: Metro (Chandni Chowk Metro Station)

What to Buy: Wedding lehengas, embroidered bags, semi-precious jewelry, silk and cotton clothes, books and electronic products

10. Greater Kailash

Greater Kailash has two sections of market known as M-Block and N-Block. The shops of these markets remain crowded for its local shopping outlets, lifestyle stores, cosmetic shops, showrooms and street food-corners. You can shop the best of casual and traditional clothes, jewelry and footwear.

How to Reach: Metro (Hauz Khas Metro Station)

What to Buy: Casual and traditional outfit, cosmetics, jewelry, lifestyle items and footw

Medical

Medical treatment is costly in Delhi if you go to a private clinic or hospital. But, there are many government hospitals which will take care of you such as Safdarjang Hospital, Lok Nayak Hospital, local free government Homeopathic clinics, etc.

Visit emergency ward of any govt. Hospital and they will give you immediate prescription. If you have to visit OPD of a govt. Hospital, try to be early by 7.30 AM, you will get a slip (numbers are allocated) and by 10 or almost 11 AM you will have an expert, doctor prescribed medicine and you will be free to go home.

Good Private hospitals:-

Fortis hospital, Max Hospital, Medanta hospital, Moolchand Hospital are private hospitals with best intensive care and treatment which automatically demands high cost.

Note: Ors.gov.in [In this site you can book appointment of any hospital and of any department. You do not need to stand on long lines.

Scam

Sometimes, people approach tourists and beg them to buy some milk in a shop for them. They will tell you something like "I need the milk for my baby" but the truth is that they made a deal with the shop and it's just a scam.

Never pay any consultant for a job, they are thugs. Most of the fake offices are situated in Janakpuri, District Centre

The auto-rickshaw scams are the most common. Either they take a longer route or don't use the meter or overcharge by the meter or they pretend they forgot to turn on the meter and charge 10x the meter amount. While traveling from Delhi to Gurgaon or Delhi to Noida or vice-versa, never ever take an auto like below because they are not allowed to cross the state border. They would tell you much lesser price compared to taxi but they will leave you at border and say change auto from here, which will cost you much more.

Never go to GB road, you will be looted. Ignore beggars at Red light, metro stations, if you give it to one, ten more will appear.

People (old, young, well dressed) will ask for ten rupees help, at random places, never help them. They are addicts.

Never sit in an unauthorised cab. You will be hypnotized and without any resistance, you will give away everything you have, cash, ATM card with pin. It's real.

Useful Legal tips

Indian Structure has offered a number of rights to the folks to guard their basic rights, however sadly, most individuals will not be conscious of their rights. I am offering some legal guidelines and the rights which not solely shield folks's pursuits but in addition ease your life.

- Motor Vehicle act, 1988 - This legislation says that if the site visitors police officer snatches the important thing from the automobile or motorbike, it's unlawful. You may have the complete proper to launch a Authorized continuing towards the officer.
- Limitation Act, 1963 - In case your workplace doesn't pay you then you might have the ability to file an FIR towards it inside 3 years. However for those who report after 3 years, you'll not get something for the due.
- Part 294 of the Indian Penal Code - In case you are discovered concerned in "obscene exercise" at a public place, you will be imprisoned for 3 months. However within the absence of a precise definition of obscene exercise police have at all times misused this act.
- Delhi Hire Management Act, 1958, Part 14 - In case you are residing in Delhi then your landlord doesn't have the best to forcefully vacate your own home with out giving prior discover to you.
- Being caught with a prostitute could result in being charged under ITPA in India which could result in 6 -

36 months of nuiscance and expenses before issue could be resolved. Caught in a brothel or parlor will result in the same consequences. However calling a girl to your own residence (rented or own) will not be deemed illegal (if girl is 18+)

- Keeping adult content on Laptop, Desktop is legal (As long as it is adult 18+), however sending mms files, transfering obscenity files, uploadin obscenity files (not downloading) is regarded under our laws as illegal and while in 99% cases nothing is done - in 1% cases action can be taken.
- For Male Persons - Even if you had consensual physical relationship with a adult woman and then broke up with her. You could be held for Cheating and Rape in India. So avoid pre-marital relationships or marry your girlfriend.
- Talking to women on obscene subjects will be termed as Sexual Harrassment in India. You may think it is flirting but it will result in a criminal record.

Tips for foreigner

1. Airport Taxi - As soon you will arrive at New Delhi airport a lot of taxi drivers will try to take you to your hotel. If you get trapped in those scams, then they will take you to some cheap quality hotels for which they get some commissions in return.

2. Auto Rickshaw - They will tell you that the place you want to go is closed due to so and so reason. And instead of taking to the place you want to go, they will take you to a specific shopping centre or shops so they can get a commission from the owner of the shop for taking you there.

3. Good looking guy - If you found a good looking guy following you and trying to talk to you or trying to be friendly or someone trying to sell something to you in and around Cp, lajpat nagar, karol bagh or pahargunj area, be cautious they may be gang of touts. You can also find them in some cafeteria or in a good looking restaurant or in a bar, wearing neat and clean cloths, looks tidy, their main motive is to cheat and become friendly with you and then their main work starts when they try to teach or guide you for official tourist information at the office of government of India. He will take you to the official govt. tourist office. These all are frauds so keep your eyes open, good presence of mind will keep you safe from the bad intentions of touts.

4.Train scams - Your booked train is cancelled, delayed, not running, and getting ripped off by touts agents with exorbitant pricing when they direct you to their so called 'agency'. These train scams are mostly active near new Delhi railway i.e paharganj, kamla market and old Delhi railway station i.e Chandni Chowk.

5. Paid blessings: Babas (Hindu holy men) will commonly approach tourists and ask if they want a blessing. They'll tie a red holy thread on your wrist and then demand a large sum of money. Also, be aware of fake sadhus who approach tourists and ask for donations. Never feel obliged to pay such an amount in any situation like this. Only give what you feel is reasonable. These scams are active near old Delhi railway station and near some temples.

6. Begging scams- It can be heart-breaking to see a "mother" with a sleepy baby in a sling begging for money at traffic lights. However these babies are often rented for the day and sedated.

7. Shopkeepers - As soon as the shop keeper sees that you're a westerner, they will get dollar signs in their eyes and jack up their prices. A simple way to avoid this is to only go to "fixed rate" shops. If this isn't possible then you will need to bargain. Learn to bargain like an Indian.

8. Be careful when exchanging money - Although exchanging money can be a risky business that scammers like to be involved with, the airport exchange places are usually fine but they do rip you off. I personally like ATM's the best because they are safest and have some of the best exchange rates.

10. SIM cards for your phone might not work - It's a little bit difficult to get sim card and typically involves a lot of paperwork and other hassles. If you don't fill out that paperwork but someone sells you a SIM, there is a good chance it's a used or defunct card that simply won't work. So better purchase sim cards from a permanent shop.

Tip: Get a local SIM card with data and get a GPS app that works offline. Do your research before arriving.

Hope, we will make our beloved Incredible India one of the best tourist destination in the world.

www.ingramcontent.com/pod-product-compliance
Lightning Source LLC
La Vergne TN
LVHW100336181026
850499LV00039B/1113